394.5

Pri
c.1

Priolo, Pauline
Piccolina and the
Easter bells

E. S. E. A.
TITLE II
PHASE TWO

DATE DUE

DORR B 4 - 2 '79		
GREN C 1 02 3 '79		
BIGS G 4 6 '81		
DORR C 1 18 '82		
GREN H 4 10 '84		
MONTA C 1 29 '86		
FORKS A 3 17 '82		

K-2   8266

It was Piccolina's heart's desire to grow
tall—but to do this she had to be lifted high
just as the Easter bells pealed!

Piccolina and the Easter Bells

PICCOLINA AND THE EASTER BELLS

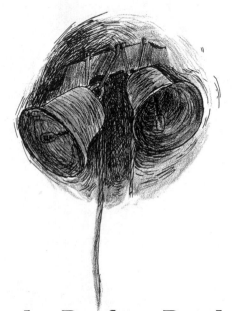

by Pauline Priolo

ILLUSTRATED BY RITA FAVA

An Atlantic Monthly Press Book

BOSTON   LITTLE, BROWN and COMPANY   TORONTO

ATLANTIC—LITTLE, BROWN BOOKS
ARE PUBLISHED BY
LITTLE, BROWN AND COMPANY
IN ASSOCIATION WITH
THE ATLANTIC MONTHLY PRESS

Published simultaneously in Canada
by Little, Brown & Company (Canada) Limited

PRINTED IN THE UNITED STATES OF AMERICA

Glossary of Sicilian Terms

La Piccolina	The little one
Biscotto (biscotti)	A sweet biscuit (biscuits)
Calia	A chick-pea, known in the United States as a *garbanzo*
Sì	Yes
Grazie	Thanks
Carrozza	Carriage
Carretta	Two-wheeled cart
Quartare	Containers to carry water
Buona Pasqua	A greeting, meaning "Happy Easter"
Shúme	A creek of running water
Stratone	Main street

To my grandchildren, Jeff and Jan

It was the day before Easter. Piccolina raced
across the kitchen floor and her bare feet were cold on
the tiles. She was thinking of the Easter bells that
would ring this morning, so children might grow tall.

7

"Mamá, today is the day of the bells," she said. "Today I will start to grow and be tall like all my friends. When all the church bells ring out the end of Lent, Papá will lift me high in the air and he will shout, 'GROW, CHILD! GROW!'"

Piccolina smelled the sweet anise seeds in the twisted Easter *biscotti* that her mother was baking. Already they filled a big bowl on the table.

"Let us hope Papá gets back in time," Mamá said. "You forget that sometimes Papá has too many passengers, which may make him late. So you must not be too sad if he doesn't get to church in time to lift you."

"But Papá *must* come in time to lift me, because

he is tall. You said yourself the higher I am lifted, the taller I will grow."

Piccolina thought of her father sitting proud and tall, driving the shiny black carriage, *la carrozza*, which carried mail and passengers to the Sicilian towns.

Just for today, Piccolina wished Papá had stayed at home. Then she could be sure he would be at the church when the Easter bells rang out for the ceremony that made children grow tall.

Last year, he had worked late, and Mamá had lifted her, but not nearly high enough. And she had not grown at all. But today, all that would be changed.

No longer would she be the smallest girl in her school. No longer would her friends call her Piccolina, the "little one." She closed her eyes tightly and wished with all her might for Papá to be on time for the bell ringing.

"Don't worry," said Mamá. "I will be at the

church.   If Papá is late I will try to lift you.   Now!''
she smiled.   "Does that make you feel better?''

Piccolina shook her head.

"You are too little, Mamá.   Last year, you couldn't
lift me as high as the other children were lifted.   And

12

I didn't grow. Papá must get to church in time to lift me. He must!"

She took a golden-brown *biscotto* from the bowl and kissed her mother.

"I'm going to church," she said.

"The bells will not ring until almost noon. You will have a long wait," said Mamá.

"I promised Tana and Peppina I would be there early. And I want to see Papá the moment he arrives."

Piccolina reached up, trying to stretch her short fingers to turn the big black iron knob, high on the kitchen door. As always, she couldn't do it with one hand.

She put down her *biscotto* and turned the big knob with both hands. Picking up her *biscotto* again, she stepped out in the morning sunshine.

Across the street, she saw Donna Rosalia holding a bowl of chicken feed, which she threw to the ground in small handfuls. A big, golden-brown rooster with a bright red comb on his head raised his wings to scare the young hens, as they rushed towards the food. The smallest hens hid in the folds of Donna Rosalia's many petticoats.

Vito, a fat young pig, stood by, watching the chickens. Piccolina saw his greedy, black eyes stare at her Easter biscuit. She knew only too well what he wanted, for this had happened before.

She raised the *biscotto* high in the air, but the pig ran straight for her. With a loud grunt, he jumped in the air and snatched the *biscotto* from her hand, knocking her to the ground. Then he ran down the street.

Piccolina quickly scrambled to her feet, while
Donna Rosalia clucked over her like a mother hen.
"Ah! Poor Piccolina!" she cried loudly, patting
Piccolina to brush the street dust from her dress.
"That Vito!" she said, shaking her head. "He never
gets enough to eat. No matter how much I feed him.
You will just have to hurry up and grow tall,
Piccolina."

Unhappily, Piccolina walked away. She was close to tears as she turned into the *stratone*. But here, in the crowded main street of the town, happy voices were calling, "*Buona Pasqua!* Happy Easter!" People were dressed in their brightest clothes. They stood talking in groups, laughing and arguing that the bells of their own church would be first to ring out the end of Lent in the ceremony of the bells. Piccolina forgot her tears and began hoping that the bells of her church would be first.

She was happy again as she pushed her way along the edge of the *stratone*.

Suddenly she felt water dripping from an iron balcony above her head. Quickly, she stepped back,

but dark wet spots formed on her dress and the dusty street as the water splashed beside her. Piccolina looked up, but all she could see was a mass of pink carnations filling the balcony.

"Oh! I'm sorry." A voice called from behind the flowers and a girl leaned over them.

Piccolina looked up at her friend Olivia.

"It's all right," she said. "It didn't really wet me."

"Oh! It's you, Piccolina," said Olivia. "You're so tiny, I hardly knew you were there!" She laughed. "Maybe you should have stood under the water. It might make you grow."

All the happiness went out of Piccolina. She

stood there, unable to say anything, because tears were filling her throat.

"Ah, don't look so sad, Piccolina," Olivia said. "You'll grow."

Piccolina moved away slowly, then walked more quickly. Tana and Peppina would be waiting for her at the church. Papá would be there, too.

"Eh! Piccolina."

She stopped short. Her uncle was standing in the doorway of his shop, where he sold sweets, coffee, sugar and *calia*—crispy, toasted beans like nuts.

She smelled the *calia* roasting in a huge pot of hot sand, which hung over the fire near the door. The beans were popping like firecrackers.

Standing on tiptoe, she felt the heat on her face, as she tried to see into the pot. Her uncle pulled her away.

"Don't get too close," he warned. "You're too little."

Even her favorite uncle reminded her of how small she was. She found it hard to smile back as Uncle Turi's short, fat body shook with friendly laughter.

"Ah, this Piccolina. She is the busy little one, this morning."

"*Sì*," she said. "I'm in a hurry. I'm on my way to meet my friends at church."

Somehow, Piccolina didn't feel like saying anything about meeting Papá.

Uncle Turi nodded.

"It must be very important. This is the first morning you have forgotten to come in for your candy."

Piccolina took the lavender-colored, sugar-coated almond from his broad palm and popped it into her mouth. It tasted like violets.

Uncle Turi gave her long braids a playful tweak.

"Run along, bright eyes," he said. "I do not wish to keep you from your important business with your friends."

Piccolina skipped down the street, happy again. She sucked sparingly on the candy, so it would last a long time.

In the town square, women were filling clay *quartare* with water at the fountain. They lifted the heavy jugs to their heads and walked away very straight and tall with their hands loose at their sides.

Now, a two-wheeled *carretta* pulled by a donkey stopped at the low watering trough beside the foun-

tain. The driver jumped to the ground and while
the donkey drank at the trough, the man drank from
the stream of water pouring out of the mouth of a
marble angel on the edge of the fountain.

Piccolina got thirsty watching him. She remem-
bered all the times she had tried to get a drink here,
so she jumped high, stretching her arms to reach the
fountain.

Her fingers closed over the wet, round edge, and she pulled herself up. She felt the cool water. Then, as always before, her fingers slipped from the smooth stone and she again stood on the dusty ground.

Piccolina started to jump again. It's no use, she thought. It will always be the same until I grow tall. She turned away.

A crowd was gathered before Piccolina's church, everyone watching the bell ringer carefully climbing to the top of the church tower. He was testing the straps that held the heavy bell that had not rung for seven weeks.

Piccolina looked for Tana and Peppina. But most of all, she looked for Papá. Slowly, she walked around the edge of the crowd. She saw children playing, but always carefully near their parents so they could be lifted high in the air when the bell rang. She saw many men, but none of them was Papá.

Piccolina pushed into the crowd to look for him. The people stood so close that it was hard to look up

and see their faces. When she looked down she could see nothing but feet. She was surrounded by feet. When she managed to squeeze her way out of the crowd, Tana and Peppina stood before her.

"Where is your Papá?" asked Peppina, smiling down at her. "I thought he was going to lift you today."

Piccolina tried not to sound worried.

"Maybe he had too many passengers," she said, remembering Mamá's warning that too many stops might make Papá late again for the bell ringing. Suddenly, Piccolina knew he would be late.

She looked up at the two tall girls and she felt as though she were shrinking and they were growing taller.

Piccolina turned and ran down the street as fast as she could run. Tana's surprised voice followed her.

"Piccolina!" she cried. "Where are you going, Piccolina?"

Her voice became an echo in Piccolina's head.

"Piccolina! Piccolina! Piccolina!" it said over and over again.

Piccolina was crying. Another whole year of being called "little one." She was sick and tired of it. Not until she reached the last house in town, where the highway into the open country began, did she stop running.

Donna Santa sat knitting on a stone bench in front of her white stone house. Her nut-brown, wrinkled old face was round with surprise.

"Ah, Piccolina!" she called. "Why aren't you near your mother today? Don't you want to grow? Soon the bells will ring."

34

Piccolina swallowed a big lump in her throat and said hopefully, "I'm waiting for *la carrozza*. Papá will lift me. If he gets back in time."

The old woman squinted her wise old eyes at the sun.

"*La carrozza* is late already, Piccolina," she said.

Piccolina walked slowly down the highway. All around her was open country. The narrow ribbon of highway lost itself over a low rise. But still she hoped to see her father driving over the low hill in his black carriage, behind the pair of fast black horses.

The sound of voices made her look to the left of the highway.

There, under the trees on the green banks of the *shúme*, stood a covered wagon. Dark-faced men sat around a campfire. Barefooted children splashed in the shallow water. Women, wearing brightly colored head scarves, stopped scrubbing clothes on the flat rocks along the creek bed of the *shúme* to stare. Their long, gold earrings flashed in the sun.

36

A tall boy walked over to Piccolina. His large black eyes were friendly as he spoke.

"What are you looking for? Are you lost?" he asked.

His voice was soft.

"I'm waiting for my Papá." Piccolina told him that the carriage was late, that Papá must have had to make too many stops, making him late for the bell ringing.

The gypsy boy listened with deep interest.

"I know how it feels to be little," he said. "I wish I could help you. It is only since I was lifted by a very tall miller when the bells rang out last year that I started to grow."

Piccolina wondered who the tall miller was. She knew only Mastro Salvatore, short and bent under a heavy sack of grain or flour whenever she saw him.

"I know!" the boy said. "I'll listen and tell you if your Papá is coming soon."

Throwing himself down, with an ear close to the ground, he listened for a moment.

"It is coming," he whispered. "I hear the horses' hoofbeats. *Una carrozza*, drawn by two fast horses."

Piccolina stared at him. What a strange power

he had. But somehow, she believed him. She wanted to believe that the carriage was bringing Papá closer and closer.

"How far away is it?" she asked. "Can you tell?"

The gypsy boy listened again, then stood up.

"I couldn't hear it any more," he said, slapping the white dust from his clothes. "But I think it stopped near the Mill."

Why, that was over the little rise in the road and the church bells could be heard from there.

"*Grazie!*" she called out, already running. She ran as fast as her legs could carry her, her feet scarcely touching the soft, dusty road. And as she reached the top of the hill, she saw the gray stone Mill below.

There was nothing on the white road. Hot tears filled her eyes and she stumbled over her own feet. Piccolina brushed the tears away with her arm. The bells weren't ringing yet. Maybe, she thought hopefully, maybe the carriage had stopped just the other side of the Mill. She ran again, faster.

Now, at the Mill, she saw a man walking slowly out of the wide doorway. He carried a large sack on his bent back and she knew it was Mastro Salvatore, the miller.

But there was no sign of Papá's carriage on the road ahead. The gypsy boy had been wrong.

She stopped beside the miller and looked up to see him smiling.

She tried to smile, but tears rolled down her cheeks.

"Piccolina, what is wrong?" asked the miller. "What are you doing out here?"

The kindness in his voice made Piccolina feel even sorrier for herself and a big sob shook her. In a shaky voice, she explained why she had come out to

meet the carriage.   Then she went on very sadly:

"And now, I will have to go another whole year being Piccolina, because Papá isn't here to lift me high and the bells will ring out any moment."

The miller smiled again.

"Don't cry, Piccolina," he said kindly.   "If your Papá isn't here in time, I can lift you."

But Piccolina cried harder, because she knew the miller would have to lift her.

For the deep, loud tone of the monastery bell rang out from the distant hills to the north.

BONG—BONG—BONG!

It rang across the wide valley, to be joined by another bell from the south, one from the east and

the last bell from the west.   All together, they rang
across the land to make the ceremony of the bells
complete.

But Papá wasn't there to lift her high in the air.
The miller let down the sack of flour from his back.

Suddenly, Piccolina stopped crying.   For the miller
began to straighten up.   She watched him stand
straight and tall.   So tall, that she had to tip back
her head to look up at his face.

Then Piccolina was so happy, she thought she would burst.

"You are even taller than Papá!" Now, she could hardly wait for the tall miller to lift her.

Then, as was the way for the ceremony of the bells, the miller cupped a hand under her chin and the other behind her head.

Piccolina felt herself lifted. High! High up in the air, while the miller shouted, "GROW, CHILD! GROW!"

Piccolina held her breath and felt herself lowered to the ground. Still the bells rang.

Again, the miller's long, strong arms lifted her into the air. So high that Piccolina felt she could

47

almost reach up and touch the white clouds in the sky!

The miller shouted again.

"GROW, CHILD! GROW!"

As Piccolina's feet touched the ground, she laughed happily. For she knew that, already, she had begun to grow.